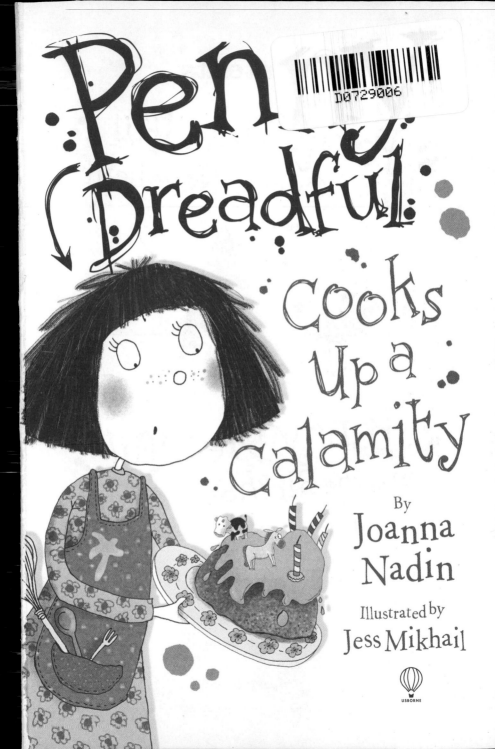

Penny Dreadful

Cooks Up a Calamity

By
Joanna
Nadin

Illustrated by
Jess Mikhail

USBORNE

Contents

Penny Dreadful
and the Field Trip
page 95

Penny Dreadful's
Top **5** Tips for Survival

page 134

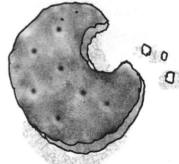

Meet Penny Dreadful and her Resigned Relations

Penny
(It's never really her fault…)

Cosmo
(Penny's best friend)

Georgia May Morton-Jones
(Penny's genius cousin)

Daisy
(Penny's annoying sister)

Penny's
long-suffering **mom** and **dad**

Very prim-and-proper
Aunt Deedee

Barry
(Meow, I'm Gran's cat)

Gran
(Normally found fast asleep somewhere)

My name is not actually Penny Dreadful. It is Penelope Jones.

The "Dreadful" part is my dad's **JOKE**. I know it is a joke because every time he says it he laughs like a honking goose. But I do not see the funny side. Plus it is not even true that I am dreadful. It is like Gran says, i.e. that I am a **MAGNET FOR DISASTER**.

Mom says if Gran kept a better eye on me in the first place instead of on *Countdown to Cook-off* then I might not be quite so magnetic. But Gran says if Mom wasn't so busy answering phones for Dr. Cement, who is her boss and who has bulgy eyes like hard-boiled eggs (which is why everyone calls him Dr. Bugeye), and Dad wasn't so busy solving crises at the city council, then they would be able to solve some crises at 73 Rollins Road, i.e. our house. So you see it is completely not my fault.

But the magnetism is extra-especially annoying when you are trying to **TURN OVER A NEW LEAF**, i.e. not be dreadful **AT ALL**, because it makes it very impossible to be sure.

What happens is that me and Gran, and

Gran's cat Barry, and my big sister Daisy (who is very irritating), are watching *Animal SOS*, which is a TV series where animals are always almost dying but then they don't and it is **MIRACULOUS**.

And this week it is all about a dog named Colin who is an **UTTER MENACE** because he is mostly digging holes and burying things in them, e.g.:

1. A pair of red pants

2. A model of Minimus Mayhem, leader of the Herobots

c. An egg whisk

Only this time he has gone a **STEP TOO FAR** and has tried to bury a toaster under some pansies,

only the toaster is still plugged in and he gets
an electric shock which makes his hair stand
on end like Hugo Brush's, who is in fifth
grade and who is named "Toilet Brush" (only
Mr. Schumann, who is our principal, says it is
not very **TOLERANT** to call people names,
but it was Hugo who started it so that is a
complete **CONUNDRUM**).

Anyway, Colin is near death and his owner Mrs. McDoon is crying into the sleeves of her red coat, and we are all on the **EDGE OF OUR SEATS** (except Barry who is eating a graham cracker, even though Mom has told Gran it is **CAT FOOD AND CAT FOOD ONLY**), when the vet gives Colin a special injection and he **MIRACULOUSLY** doesn't die but sits up and licks a computer. And Griff Hunt, who is the presenter, says he hopes

Colin has learned his lesson, and Mrs. McDoon says he has and he will definitely **TURN OVER A NEW LEAF**. Although this is possibly not true because Colin is looking very much like he wants to bury the computer under the floor. But Griff Hunt ignores this and says Colin is **INSPIRING**, which **IS** true because then we are all very **INSPIRED**, i.e. Gran says she is **TURNING OVER A NEW LEAF** and is not going to let Barry eat graham crackers any more,

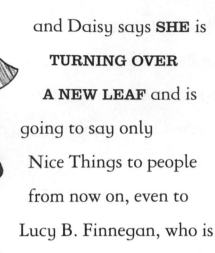

and Daisy says **SHE** is **TURNING OVER A NEW LEAF** and is going to say only Nice Things to people from now on, even to Lucy B. Finnegan, who is normally her best friend (only this week Lucy is best friends with Patricia Rigby-Homerton, who has a TV in her bedroom and Mom says no, Daisy cannot have one, not **EVEN** over her dead body).

And I think I would also like to **TURN OVER A NEW LEAF** and it would be pretty nice not to be shouted at, so I say I am absolutely **NOT** going to be **DREADFUL** any more.

Only Daisy says,

You are an **UTTER MORON** if you think that is going to happen. Pigs are more likely to fly.

But Gran says Daisy's leaf has turned back over already because that was not a Nice Thing, so it is one point to me.

And on Friday it is clear Mr. Schumann has also watched *Animal SOS* because usually he is **SICK AND TIRED** of a lot of things, especially me, e.g.,

Penelope Jones, I am **SICK AND TIRED** of telling you to stop trying to burn things with a magnifying glass. I do **NOT** want to call the fire department out again.

Because me and Cosmo Moon Webster, who is my best friend (even though he is a week older than me and a boy), are really into burning things with a magnifying glass, e.g.:

a) An old log

b) A dead ant

3. Bridget Grimes, who is the star student in class and Mr. Schumann's favorite

Only today in assembly Mr. Schumann is surprisingly not being **SICK AND TIRED** of me showing Cosmo a gold pirate coin I found outside the general store (only Cosmo says it is not a pirate coin, it is a chocolate sovereign), he is smiling and saying that on Monday in assembly we will be having a special **TALENT SHOW** and anyone can enter, even me.

Which is good because normally I am not allowed onstage because of the time I was Little Lord Jesus in our nativity and did some realistic crying, only Bridget Grimes did not think my crying was realistic, she thought it was annoying because no one could hear her sing "Away in a Manger" and so **SHE** started crying, which Mr. Schumann **DID** think was realistic, and also annoying, and also **MY FAULT**.

Anyway, it is completely clear that Mr. Schumann has **TURNED OVER A NEW LEAF**. And I am very **INSPIRED** by this and so is everyone in our class, because when we get back from assembly everyone is shouting like **CRAZY** about what talents they are going to do in the show, e.g.:

a) Luke Bruce is going to make a poodle out of balloons.

b) Alexander Pringle, who is mostly eating jelly sandwiches when he should **NOT** be eating jelly sandwiches, is going to show everyone the mole on his leg, which is in the shape of a gnu.

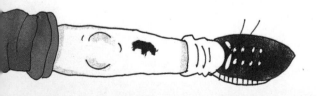

3) Bridget Grimes is going to play "If I Had A Hammer" on her recorder, and she has not **ONCE** gotten a note wrong.

d. Cosmo Moon Webster

is going to do a sun dance, because his mom Sunflower (whose real name is Barbara) is not okay with talent shows because they are **COMMERCIAL** and **COMPETITIVE**, but she **IS** very okay with sun dances.

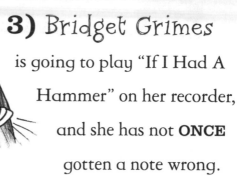

v) Henry Potts, who is Cosmo's mortal enemy, says he is going to do a rain dance, which will **OBLITERATE** Cosmo's sun dance.

6) Cosmo says he is going to do a lightning dance, which will **OBLITERATE** Henry's rain dance.

Miss Patterson, who is our teacher, and who is tall and thin like a beanpole, says it would be better if they saved their energy for dancing **NOT** arguing, and also that a mole is not a talent and that Alexander Pringle will have to think of something better, and so he says he is going play "If I Had A Hammer" on his recorder. Only Bridget Grimes says that is **COPYING** and starts crying that he is going to win the prize of a million dollars and it is **NOT FAIR**. Only Miss Patterson says the prize is **NOT** a million dollars, it is a raffia owl and the **JOY** of knowing you have won.

Only Henry Potts says he already has a raffia owl and can the prize be a lightsaber instead and less joy? And I say that would be unfair because I do not want a lightsaber because I am banned from them for several reasons. But Henry Potts says I will not win anyway because I do not have a talent. And I say,

And he says,

And I say,

So he says,

And I say it is an **AMAZING** talent and also
SECRET because I do not want to be copied
by Alexander Pringle. And Henry Potts
says I am a **LIAR**. And I say I am not, it is
just so **SECRET** that even I do not know
what it is yet. So Henry says I am **CRAZY**.

And Cosmo throws an eraser at him, which is when Miss Patterson says **NO ONE** is crazy and **EVERYONE** has talent but that **NO ONE** is going to win any prizes, not even joy and a raffia owl, unless we **PIPE DOWN** and open up our math books.

So I am utterly racking my brain to discover my secret and amazing talent, only I am not discovering anything at all, especially not the answer to "How many buckets of water does it take to fill a bathtub?" (which if you think about it **IS** crazy because that is what faucets are for). But also I am so busy racking my brain that I do not swing on my chair **OR** flick things at Bridget Grimes, so I am not **DREADFUL** and so my new leaf is definitely **TURNING**.

Only when I get home I **STILL** do not know what my secret and amazing talent is and nor does anyone else. Daisy says it is "Being a moron" and Dad does the honking goose laugh, but I do not see the funny side. And nor does Mom who says,

Penelope is trying **VERY** hard to turn over a new leaf, **UNLIKE** Daisy, and if you can't say something helpful, Gordon, don't say anything at all.

So Daisy says she is going upstairs to lie on her bed and mope (which is her most favorite activity ever since Mom said she was not allowed a TV in her bedroom not **EVEN** over her dead body), and Dad says, "Did I ever tell you I could have been an Olympic high jumper if I hadn't met your mother." And Mom says, "That is **NOT** what I was thinking of, Gordon, and no you couldn't

because you trip over even a twig." Which is true because right then Dad tries to high jump, only he trips over the carpet and knocks a big book about bees off the coffee table, which falls on the remote control, which turns off the TV, which is very **DISCOMBOBULATING** for Gran (who has been watching *Animal SOS* about a cow who is trapped in an old phone booth) who thinks it is maybe magic.

Only Mom says there is no such thing as magic, only **COINCIDENCE**. But Gran says there **IS** such a thing as **MAGIC** because her friend Arthur Peason was a magician called The Great Horrendous, before he got old and bald, and can in fact make rabbits jump out of a hat and also saw people in half. Which is when I have my **BRILLIANT IDEA™**, which is that **MAGIC** can be my secret and amazing talent and it is **SO** amazing that I will definitely win the raffia owl and the joy and also **TURN OVER A NEW LEAF**.

So the next day after
school, me and Cosmo
and Gran go to see
Arthur Peason

and he puts on his special cloak and hat with silvery stars on it and I am his glamorous assistant and I get inside a special box and he completely saws me in half (because he does not have any rabbits to jump out of a hat anymore). Only he does not **ACTUALLY** saw me, he just saws some wood while I am tucked up in a secret compartment.

And then he lets me put on the cloak and hat and I saw Cosmo in half. And then Cosmo says maybe he will not do a sun dance and will be my glamorous assistant instead. Only Arthur Peason says it is very important to have a volunteer from the audience and it absolutely must be a beautiful lady because then the crowd will be on the **EDGE OF THEIR SEATS** and will "ooh" and "aah" a lot more, which is not magic, it is scientific fact.

And then we go home with the box and the
saw and the hat and the cloak and I ask Mom
to get in the box because she is a beautiful lady,
although she is not very voluntary because she
says she would very much like to remain in
ONE PIECE rather than be sawn in two. Only I

say she will not be sawn in two because of the secret compartment and I am right, and so is Arthur Peason because everyone is on the edge of their seats, especially Dad, and they all "ooh" and "aah" and Mom is utterly **NOT** sawn, she is **IN ONE PIECE**, and I am pleased as punch because my leaf has definitely **TURNED**.

And on Monday I am so **CRAZY** with excitement about my secret and amazing talent that I cannot even sit still, and Mr. Schumann has to say, "Penelope Jones, seats are for bottoms, not for balancing," but he does not say he is **SICK AND TIRED** so his new leaf is still turned, even though:

a) Henry Potts has done his rain dance and he has used real rain (i.e. some water bottles with holes) and there is water on Bridget Grimes's recorder and so she has had to wait a turn until it is all dry, and

2. Alexander Pringle has done his talent, which is not his mole or the recorder, it is fitting marshmallows in his mouth and it is fourteen, only they have fallen out and made a sticky mess on the floor and Mr. Eggs, who is our janitor and who smells like dogs, has had to come and clean it all up.

I say,

Do not worry, Mr. Schumann, because it is my turn next and there is no water or sticky and also I will not be on my seat at all, I will be **AMAZING** you with my secret talent.

And then it is Mr. Schumann's turn to be on the edge of his seat because I am in my hat and cloak and saying, "I am The Great Cornetto and I am going to saw somebody in half MAGICALLY." Only Mr. Schumann says he does not want anyone being sawn as it is against school rules and also the law. Only I tell him I will not actually saw them because of the secret compartment. And Mr. Schumann checks the secret compartment and says it is definitely there, so I can do some sawing.

And so I say, "I need a volunteer and they must be beautiful and glamorous," and everyone is going "Me, me" and waving their hands in the air.

Only I do not
think that Cherry
Scarpelli is very
GLAMOROUS
because she is
dressed like a
monkey because
her talent is a song
from *The Jungle Book*.

And I do not think
Alexander Pringle is very
GLAMOROUS because he is
covered in marshmallows,
and also he is not a lady.

And in fact the most **GLAMOROUS** person who is also a lady is Bridget Grimes, because she is wearing a purple dress and also she has long hair that actually reaches her waist and she is always swooshing it and saying "My hair actually reaches my waist, Penelope Jones," only Mom says it needs a good cut. But for once I do not agree because it will be very **GLAMOROUS** when it is hanging out of the box, so I pick her.

And so Bridget is in the box and I am waving my saw and saying,

And now I will utterly and completely saw Bridget Grimes in half before your **VERY EYES**.

And it is completely **MAGIC** because I do the

sawing and everyone says,

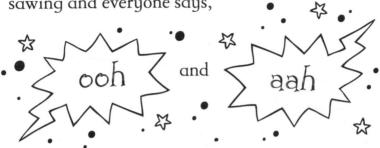

ooh and aah

like **CRAZY** and she is completely in **TWO PIECES**.

And then I put her back again and she is

in **ONE PIECE**.

Only that is when the ⟨BAD THING™⟩ happens, which is that I absolutely cannot open the box. And nor can Mr. Schumann, and nor can Miss Patterson, and nor can Mr. Eggs.

And so Mr. Schumann has to call the fire department and they do **ACTUAL** sawing to get Bridget Grimes out and there is more "ooh"ing and "aah"ing than ever, and also Bridget Grimes is screaming massively in case they chop her head off with her long hair.

But at last she is **FREE** and everyone claps and the firemen do a bow and everyone is pleased as punch. Except Mr. Schumann, whose leaf has definitely turned the wrong way again because he says he is **SICK AND TIRED** of calling the fire department, it is the third time this year,

and I say it is not, it is two, and he says it is definitely three, i.e.:

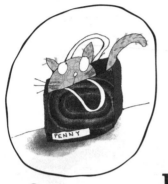

1. The time I brought Barry in for show-and-tell and he ran up the curtains in the cafeteria and got stuck and had to be rescued.

b) The time me and Elsie Maud, who was a new girl but only for a week, got Alexander Pringle to reach a dead pigeon on the other side of the railings and he got his head stuck and had to be rescued.

c) Today.

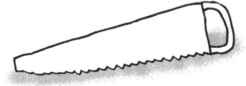

And so he is completely right, which means I am disqualified from the talent show **AND** I am banned from being onstage until I can prove I am responsible, which means I will not get to be a corn on the cob in the Harvest Festival and wear a helmet made of yellow felt. And it means my new leaf has definitely turned back into an old one.

And so has Daisy's, because she is best friends with Lucy B.

Finnegan again since Patricia's TV has been confiscated until she can get at least a B in science, which means Daisy does not have to say Nice Things, she can say what she likes, which right now is,

It is all your fault, Penelope Jones, you are such a **COMPLETE MORON**.

And Dad calls me Penny Dreadful and does the honking goose laugh, and Mom does not see the funny side.

But for once I do see it. Because even though I do not win, nor does Bridget Grimes, because she is very trembly after the sawing and gets four notes wrong in "If I Had A Hammer" and so she does not show off for at least a week. In fact it is Cosmo who wins with his sun dance, which Mr. Schumann says is at least "dry and clean."

And even though I am not Cosmo's glamorous assistant, I am utterly his best friend, and so he says I can share half his joy and have the raffia owl every other weekend.

Penny Dreadful

and the

Birthday Wish

Mostly I do not see the point of wishes because they absolutely almost **NEVER** come true. For instance, so far this year I have wished for:

a) A butterscotch ice cream that never melts

b) A Tyrannosaurus rex

3. A pair of X-ray glasses

4. A time machine (for Cosmo's birthday because he is very big on time machines, especially ones made out of a bus, some tinfoil and an alarm clock)

v) $67.82

And I did not get a butterscotch ice cream that never melts, or a pair of X-ray glasses or a Tyrannosaurus rex. And Cosmo did not get his time machine, he got some licorice sticks and a pen in the shape of a vampire.

But he was pleased as punch anyway because
Henry Potts, who is his mortal enemy, has a
pen in the shape of a werewolf and Cosmo
says vampires are more deadly than
werewolves and his pen would obliterate Henry
Potts's pen, which it did, only Miss Patterson
was not very happy about all the ink on the
floor, which Cosmo said was werewolf blood,

which made Bridget Grimes
cry because she thinks
werewolves are real
(but I have checked
with Mr. Schumann
and they are not, they
are only on television
and in London).

But I am **NOT** pleased as punch, especially about the $67.82 because that is how much I owe Mom for a lot of reasons, e.g.:

1. The time I accidentally called India.

b) The time we broke Dad's razor by shaving Georgia May Morton-Jones's head, which had superglue on it.

iii) The time me and Cosmo broke the vacuum cleaner by sucking up some bubbles.

And I will be paying her back **UNTIL KINGDOM COME**, only I wish it would come quickish because it is Mom's birthday **TODAY** and I need $6.99 to buy her a mug with a picture of a monkey on it that is in the window at the general store, so I can give it to her at her **BIRTHDAY DINNER** later.

Mom says she would rather just have some **PEACE** and **QUIET** because at that **EXACT** moment Daisy and Lucy B. Finnegan are standing on the table pretending to be international horse riders receiving Olympic medals for jumping over some red and white planks and they are **LOUD**, and Gran is watching the news,

which is about some bombs exploding which

are very **LOUD**, and Barry the cat is

howling (only it is not

because of the bombs

but because he does not

like the man who does the news) and he is

rather **LOUD**, and I am saying,

But if you do not lend me some money then I cannot buy you a present and you will be doubly upset with me and so you see it is completely not my fault.

And I am saying it rather **LOUD**. So Mom says she is just glad that Dad is still out at work solving a crisis to do with a traffic circle because at least it is one less noise to add to the **CACOPHONY**. Which is when Dad walks in and adds his noise to the **CACOPHONY** by saying,

The traffic circle is fixed, no thanks to Kenny Jupiter. Honestly, he has baked beans for brains — oh and I hope you don't mind but I have invited Deedee over for your **BIRTHDAY DINNER** later and it will be absolutely fun, you will see.

Only I think that possibly Mom **WILL NOT** see and she **WILL** mind because Aunt Deedee is almost **NEVER** fun and almost **ALWAYS** getting upset with me or Mom or Gran, e.g. for accidentally letting Georgia May Morton-Jones, who is my cousin and who is four and goes to The Greely Academy for Girls, eat mud.

And I am right because Mom says she **WISHES** Dad would learn to think before he speaks or that a fairy godmother would appear

and whisk her away to Timbuktu or even just to Fairview, as long as it is very far from all this **HOO-HA**. But until that happens she is going to the hairdresser's for a **BIRTHDAY TRIM** and Shaniqua Reynolds had better not be **OVERAMBITIOUS**. And I am about to say that statistically I do not think her **WISH** will happen because I have still not gotten my Tyrannosaurus or the butterscotch ice cream that never melts or a pair of X-ray glasses, only then I remember about the **PEACE** and **QUIET** so I go to Cosmo's house instead.

Cosmo's house is good because his mom, who is called Sunflower (even though her real name is Barbara), does not believe in **PEACE** and **QUIET**, she believes in **FREE SPEECH** because it is Cosmo's **HUMAN RIGHT**, even if the speech is being Darth Vader and saying *"I am Darth Vader and I am going to smite you with my omnipotent powers"* a hundred and forty-three times (which is what he did last Sunday). But today he is not into being Darth Vader, he is into trading an eraser in the shape of a weasel for my Dogs of the World poster. This is because at school everyone is **CRAZY** for trading, e.g.:

a) Alexander Pringle has traded a jelly sandwich for Luke Bruce's peanut butter cracker.

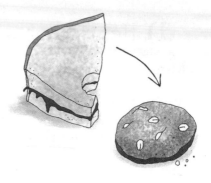

b) Bridget Grimes has traded a broken doll for Cherry Scarpelli's plastic pony with its tail cut off.

3. Brady O'Grady has traded a shiny fifty cent piece for Denzil

Wellington's one dollar coin with a dent in it.

d) Henry Potts has traded Minimus Mayhem, leader of the Herobots, for Jamal Malik's little brother Shoaib, only Shoaib is not very happy about this and nor is Mrs. Malik and nor is Mr. Schumann, who decides to ban trades at school until we can learn what is tradeable and what is not.

So I say I will not trade my Dogs of the World poster for Cosmo's eraser in the shape of a weasel but I **WILL** trade a can of sardines that is past its use-by date (and which Gran was going to give to Barry) for the eraser, and Cosmo says yes

because the can might be an antique and worth a fortune e.g. $100 in five years' time, and we can go on TV and everyone will **GASP** and wish they had kept their can of sardines.

And I say it is a shame it is not five years' time now because then I could sell the can of sardines and pay Mom back $67.82 **AND** buy her the mug with the monkey on it from the general store as it is only $6.99. Which is when Cosmo has a

BRILLIANT IDEA™,

which is to not **BUY** the mug but to **TRADE** something for it with Mrs. Butterworth, who works in the general store and who has a mustache and a beady eye (which I know because she is mostly saying "I have got my beady eye on you, Penelope Jones").

So we are investigating Cosmo's **WORLDLY POSSESSIONS**, i.e. the contents of his cabinet with the wonky handle, for something good to trade and we find seven things and they are:

1. A pair of stilts made out of flowerpots

2. Buckingham Palace on a key ring

c) A dried toad

d) A snow globe of Rapunzel that is leaky and all the snow is on the carpet

V. Three baby teeth

6. A book about deadly beasts with a free glow-in-the-dark snake ring

g) A spy pen which uses invisible ink and you have to shine a flashlight on it to see what is written and once we wrote *"Henry Potts eats roly polies"* on his spelling book and Henry **STILL** hasn't seen it, which Cosmo says is **BRILLIANT** but I say is disappointing because where is the fun in **THAT**?

Cosmo says Mrs. Butterworth will not want the snow globe of Rapunzel that is leaky with all the snow on the carpet, or three baby teeth, or a book about deadly beasts with a free glow-in-the-dark snake ring. Which means she is **CRAZY**, because who would **NOT** want a book about beasts with a free glow-in-the-dark snake ring?

Anyway it turns out she is **DOUBLY CRAZY**, because she also does not want the pair of stilts made out of flowerpots **OR** the Buckingham Palace on a key ring **OR** the dried toad **OR** the spy pen with invisible ink, and in fact she does not want to trade the mug with the monkey on it that is only $6.99

for **ANYTHING**, except $6.99 in **ACTUAL** money and **NOT** in foreign coins. And Cosmo says,

which is when you write down, e.g.:

I OWE you four pieces of cold flavored bubble gum

on a piece of paper and give it to Alexander
Pringle. Only Alexander Pringle says he is not
falling for that again because Cosmo still owes
him for the gum, and Mrs. Butterworth says
SHE is not falling for that again because Mr.
Nugent still owes her for a first-class stamp and
a box of wintergreen mints and she will never
get that back because he perished in 1997. I say
I am absolutely **NOT** going to perish but Mrs.
Butterworth gives me a look with her beady eye
that could quite possibly perish me anyway,

so me and Cosmo are back at **SQUARE ONE**
(which is also called Cosmo's house).

And we are lying on his rug made out of
recycled shopping bags and saying,

It is **NOT FAIR**!

quite a bit when Sunflower comes in, and she is very **BIG** on fairness so we tell her about the **BIRTHDAY DINNER** and Timbuktu and the mug with the monkey on it (which is only $6.99), only Sunflower says a mug with a monkey on it is **NOT** a good present because it is a **BOUGHT** present and all the best presents are ones that are made with **LOVE** or recycled shopping bags.

But Cosmo says we do not **HAVE** any recycled shopping bags because she made them into a poncho last week, so it will have to be **LOVE**. Only I say it will have to be some **LOVE** that does not involve scissors or glue because I am **BANNED** from them for several reasons. And Sunflower says in that case I can bake my **LOVE** into a **CAKE**, which will make Mom utterly pleased and she will not want to go to Timbuktu **OR** Fairview and we can make it right here which is **FORTUITOUS** because I am not allowed to use the oven at our house.

But what is **NOT FORTUITOUS** is that Sunflower does not believe in **RECIPES** because they are like **RULES** and rules are against her **HUMAN RIGHTS** and she says we have to use our

IMAGINATIONS and invent a **CAKE OF DREAMS**.
So what we do is we get a giant bowl and in it we
put several things from the cabinet, i.e.:

1. A bag of flour

b. A box of eggs

c. A jar of dark syrup

4. Some cubes of lime gelatin, cut up

5. A package of chocolate chips

f. Some grated cheese (because Mom is
always saying that grated cheese is the **ICING
ON THE CAKE** of **ANY** food, but we put it
INSIDE the cake because we want to put pink
stuff and some plastic farm animals on top).

And that is when I have my

which is to put a coin inside the cake too and
it will be like finding a lucky penny and
whoever gets it will be able to make a special
wish, e.g. for a year's supply of graham
crackers, and Cosmo says that is definitely a

BRILLIANT IDEA™

Only we cannot find a coin

so we have to use a plastic piglet

instead, but Cosmo says it is definitely a lucky

piglet because it only has three legs but it can

still stand up, which is a **MIRACLE**.

So then we go to the backyard and ask

Sunflower to turn the oven on (because she is

doing yoga by the compost pile and because we

are being **RESPONSIBLE** and also because

Cosmo does not know which knob is **ON**),

and we put the cake inside for

almost about an hour which is

when Cosmo says it must

definitely be absolutely

cooked by now.

And he is right because mostly it has risen up like **CRAZY**, except for the middle which is very sunken and also a bit gloopy, plus the three-legged piglet is upside down in it and it looks like it has drowned in some mud, but Cosmo says we will cover that up with the pink stuff and no one will be **ANY THE WISER**.

And he is right again, because we put on loads of pink stuff, which is made from butter and sugar and cranberry juice for the pink (because Sunflower does not believe in **ARTIFICIAL COLORING**), and we stick a cow and a horse with one eye on top and it looks **MAGNIFICENT** and is utterly a **CAKE OF DREAMS**.

And then we carry it completely carefully all the way back to my house for the **BIRTHDAY DINNER**.

And when we get there Mom is already looking utterly gloomy and also very strange because Shaniqua Reynolds has definitely been **OVERAMBITIOUS** and now her hair is definitely shorter on one side than the other and Dad is saying,

Only Mom says,

It is not so bad and in fact if you lean to the left all the time you almost look normal.

Gordon, if you cannot say anything helpful then do not say anything at all.

So then he is utterly quiet. But someone is **NOT** utterly quiet and that is Aunt Deedee who says,

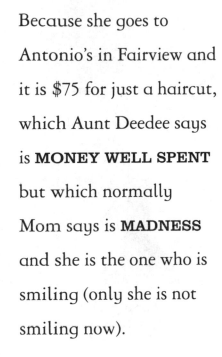

Well if you go to **CHEAP** places you have only **YOURSELF** to blame.

Because she goes to Antonio's in Fairview and it is $75 for just a haircut, which Aunt Deedee says is **MONEY WELL SPENT** but which normally Mom says is **MADNESS** and she is the one who is smiling (only she is not smiling now).

So then Dad says, "Maybe it is present time," and everyone agrees and so Mom opens her presents, which are:

1. Some oven gloves from Dad.

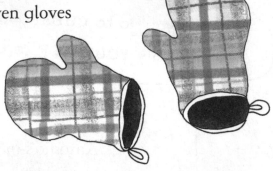

b) A purple scarf from Daisy because purple is Daisy's favorite color this week.

c) Violet bubble bath from Gran.

4. A book about birds from Barry.

5. A ticket to a concert by Mr. Nakamura (who is Georgia May Morton-Jones's music teacher and says she shows potential on the violin) from Aunt Deedee.

And Daisy says,

What is your present, Penelope Jones? I bet it is **MORONIC**.

And I say, "It is **NOT**, it is a **CAKE OF DREAMS** and it is the best kind of present because it is made with **LOVE**, and also eggs and some other stuff, and here it is — **TA-DA**!" And me and Cosmo bring in the **CAKE OF DREAMS** and put it on the table.

And Daisy says,

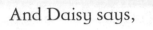

Why is there a
horse with one eye
on top?

And Cosmo says,

It is **DECORATION**,
and also there is a
three-legged pig inside
and whoever gets it
can make a wish.

And Dad says,

Wonderful. What a
BRILLIANT IDEA™!

Only Mom is not looking as if she thinks it is completely **BRILLIANT** but that is only because she has not tasted it yet, so I say,

It is time to cut the cake!

And so Dad does it because I am not allowed to use a knife ever since the time I sliced a very little bit of my thumb off. And there is a piece

for everyone except Barry
(because Mom says it is **CAT
FOOD AND
CAT FOOD ONLY**).

Only Aunt Deedee
possibly wishes there
wasn't a piece for her
because almost immediately
she turns very palish and then
very reddish and it is clear
she is **CHOKING**.

And so Cosmo says,

Do not fear,
I will come to your
rescue, I am your
**KNIGHT IN SHINING
ARMOR**.

Because he is very into being a knight in shining armor (as well as Darth Vader). And he hits her very hard on the back, which is when the three-legged piglet flies out and hits Dad on the nose.

And then there is all sorts of **KERFUFFLE**
and Aunt Deedee is completely upset and goes
home to be **REVIVED** with a bubble bath and
an aspirin and then there is shouting of,

It is **YOUR** fault!

No, it is **YOUR** fault!

And especially that it is **MY** fault because I am
such a **COMPLETE MORON** and it is the worst
birthday **EVER** (it is Daisy who says that).

But **AMAZINGLY**
Mom does not agree and
she is smiling, even though
her hair is wonky.
And she says in fact it is the **BEST**
birthday ever because she
got her **WISH**, which is
that Aunt Deedee would
BE QUIET and **GO HOME**. And I
absolutely agree that it is the
BEST BIRTHDAY EVER because at that exact
moment Dad finds another present under the
table and he says, "Oh, is
this from you too, Penny?"
And I say, "No." And he says,
"Yes it is, it says so here."

And Mom opens it and it is the mug with the monkey on it from the general store and Dad gives me a wink and I give him a wink back and I think that maybe wishes **DO** come true after all.

Penny Dreadful

and the

Field Trip

DO NOT OPEN

• mummified Cat

Mr. Schumann is
our principal and
he is mostly saying
things like "Penelope
Jones, I am **SICK**
and **TIRED** of telling
you to stop putting that
pencil up your nose,"

which is not even true because it was a pen and plus I was only seeing if I could get the raisin out that was stuck in there from lunchtime, which I could, so it was a **GOOD THING**. But he is also saying something else absolutely a lot, which is "The world is **FULL OF WONDER** so you must be **FULL OF WONDER** too."

And mostly me and Cosmo Moon Webster are not in agreement with him, because we do not see what is so **WONDERFUL** about our town which does not have, e.g.:

1. A mysterious and ancient burial ground
b) Smugglers
c) A Tyrannosaurus rex
4. Darth Vader

Instead it has a park with a broken swing (from when me and Cosmo were doing an experiment to see how many people could fit on it before it broke and it was four), a dead pigeon that has been behind the general store for two weeks and no one has moved it, and single lane streets throughout town that Dad says **DEFY LOGIC**.

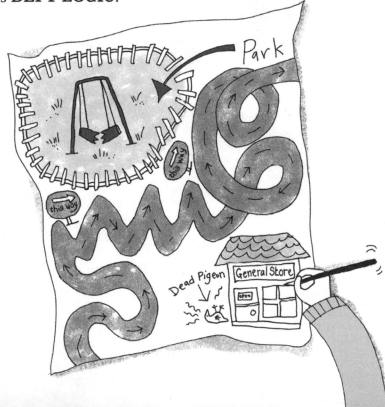

And so I tell Miss Patterson,
who is our teacher and who is
tall and thin like a beanpole, that
my world is absolutely **NOT** full of
WONDER and that in fact
it **DEFIES LOGIC**, but she says
Mr. Schumann was not
talking about this exact
town, and that I need
to look further than **IN
FRONT OF MY EYES**
and I will see all sorts
of interesting things,
e.g. the **WONDERS
OF THE WORLD** and
there are seven of them.

And then everyone is arguing like **CRAZY** about what the **WONDERS OF THE WORLD** are, i.e.:

1. Bridget Grimes says one is the Queen of England's Palace.

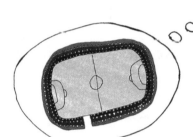

2. Brady O'Grady says one is Bayburn Stadium.

c) Henry Potts says one is Alexander Pringle, because he wears size 14 clothes even though he is nine (which is because of his glands, and also the eating).

d) Cosmo says one is Henry Potts's brain because it is so small, even smaller than a flea, and not even a microscope can see it.

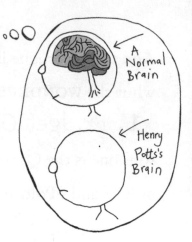

A Normal Brain

Henry Potts's Brain

But Miss Patterson says we are all wrong because in fact they are:

a) The Hanging Gardens of Babylon

b) The Great Pyramid of Giza

3. The Mausoleum of Halicarnassus

iv) The Temple of Artemis

5. The Colossus of Rhodes

f) The Statue of Zeus

7. The Lighthouse of Alexandria

And we are going to see one of them on a **SCHOOL FIELD TRIP** tomorrow and it is a **PYRAMID** and almost immediately I am **FULL OF WONDER** because I am very **BIG** on pyramids, especially the **CURSE OF THE MUMMIES**, which means that when you go into a mummy's tomb they put an ancient **CURSE** on you and you will **PERISH**, which I tell Miss Patterson.

Only then Bridget Grimes
starts crying because
she does not want to
be cursed by the
mummies and
perish, and Cherry
Scarpelli is crying
because she does not

want to go to Egypt and get an upset tummy

like she did in Bora Bora last
year, and Brady O'Grady is
crying because Alexander
Pringle stomped on his
foot because Brady said
Alexander was the
Colossus of St. Regina's.

Which is when Miss Patterson says to all stop being **SILLY** because **NO ONE** is going to **EGYPT** and **NO ONE** is going to get **CURSED** because we are going to the Museum of Natural History to look at a piece of sarcophagus and a mummified cat and some photos of the Great Pyramid and it is five dollars for the bus and you must wear **STRICT UNIFORM AND UNIFORM ONLY** and

also get your mom or dad to sign the special form or you will be staying behind to pick up litter with Mr. Eggs (who is our janitor and who smells like dogs).

And so when I get home I tell Mom about the **WORLD OF WONDER** and that she absolutely has to sign the special form and give me five dollars (especially because Mr. Eggs does not like me since the time I accidentally clogged the sink by trying to wash some rice away). And Mom says,

Hmmm, I suppose it will be mind-expanding, but there will have to be **RULES**, Penelope Jones.

And they are:

1. No **SHENANIGANS** on the bus
2. No getting **LOST**
c) No **TOUCHING** artifacts, which are
old and ancient things in museums

Because she does **NOT** want to be paying for
more **BREAKAGES**, because she has only just
finished paying the man at the Chocolate
Museum for the time I ate a piece of the Caramel
Crunch Leaning Tower of Pisa, which in fact was
not my fault, it was Cosmo's, because he is the
one who said it would make it less leany. Only
I do not say this, I say **YES** I will **NOT** do any
of those things, and so she signs the form.

Daisy says,

You are **CRAZY** if you think she will not get up to **SHENANIGANS** because she is utterly a **MORON** when it comes to museums.

But I say I will not be a moron because I will be too busy being **FULL OF WONDER** and she is just jealous because she wishes **SHE** was going to look at artifacts instead of doing double math with Mr. Munnings, who has hairy hands.

And Daisy says that is not true and I say **IS** and she says **IS NOT** and I say **IS** and we do that a lot until Mom says she wishes **SHE** was going to look at artifacts instead of looking after all of us, which is a **THANKLESS TASK**. And then Dad says he wishes **HE** was going to look at artifacts instead of having a meeting about the yellow lines outside the Scout Hut, which are causing all sorts of hoo-ha with the Cub Scout leaders, because that is a **THANKLESS TASK**. And Gran says she wishes **SHE** was coming to look at artifacts instead of playing rummy with Arthur Peason because that is a **THANKLESS TASK** because he always cheats. Which is when Mom says that none of us understand the meaning of **THANKLESS**, and to please stop the artifact nonsense because she has had it **UP TO HERE** today, what with Dr. Cement and his broken door handle, which meant he got trapped in his office with Mrs. Nougat and her bunions for an **HOUR**. So then we are all as quiet as **MICE** and no one mentions artifacts again, not **EVEN** in a whisper.

But the next morning when I go to school everyone is **CRAZY** with **EXCITEMENT** about the artifacts, except Luke Bruce who has forgotten his form and so it is litter-picking with

Mr. Eggs for him. Miss Patterson says it is also litter-picking for Cosmo because he is not in **STRICT UNIFORM**, only Cosmo says he has his form and it **IS** signed and so is a letter from his mom Sunflower which says that she does not believe in **UNIFORM** because it is oppressive and made of polyester, and she believes in **FREEDOM** and **SELF-EXPRESSION** and also natural fibers, which is why he is wearing a turban and a big cloak.

And Miss Patterson does not have anything to say to that, which is a **GOOD THING**, because if she did, Sunflower would have a one-woman sit-in protest because she is very **BIG** on them (but Miss Patterson and Mr. Schumann are not).

And also because at that very minute Dwayne
Eggs, who is the son of Mr. Eggs (but does not
smell like dogs), arrives driving the bus, and it is
NOT the old one that smells like dogs, it is a **NEW**
one called the Speedy Superbus and it has a
machine for drinks and one for
chips and a toilet and a
shower and a sprinkler
system in case of **FIRE**
and a stop lever in case
of **EMERGENCIES** and
in fact Dwayne Eggs says
it is a **WONDER OF
THE WORLD.**

Only Bridget Grimes says no it is not, because she has learned them all by heart and she will tell him if he wants, only Dwayne Eggs does not want, and nor does Mr. Schumann, who says it is time to climb on board and that we must absolutely be on our **BEST BEHAVIOR** or we will let all sorts of people down, e.g.:

a) Miss Patterson

2. St. Regina's

c) OURSELVES

And he looks especially at me at that part. I say,

"*I have* **NEVER** *let myself down.*" And Mr. Schumann says, "*Two out of three is bad enough.*" But I do not understand what he means so instead I just climb on board and Miss Patterson counts us all and there are twenty-seven and Mr. Schumann says there had better be twenty-seven on the way back or it will be **CURTAINS** for field trips.

So at last we are **OFF** and Mr. Schumann was right because I am absolutely **FULL OF WONDER** and it is at the Speedy Superbus. And I am wondering whether to have a shower first or get a can of lemonade and Cosmo says it is best to have the lemonade first because then if I make a mess I can shower the lemony all off.

And it is completely **FORTUITOUS** because
Mom has given me three dollars, only it is to
get something from the museum gift shop with
or for **EMERGENCIES**, but I think the
lemonade is maybe an **EMERGENCY** because
I am super-thirsty and Cosmo has used my
water to make a swimming pool for a fly which
is on the floor.

So I put my coin in the slot, only a can of
lemonade **DOES NOT** come out.
Which completely **DEFIES LOGIC**
and is also a definite
EMERGENCY, so I think
I had better pull the
EMERGENCY
STOP LEVER,

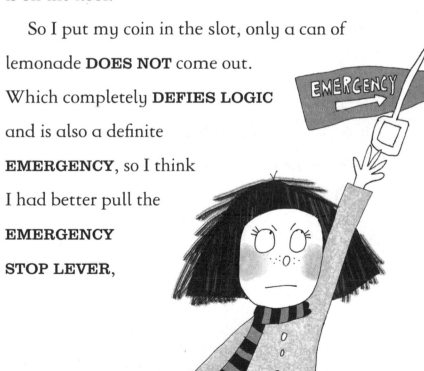

only at that exact moment Bridget Grimes appears and she says, "*I would not do that if I were you, Penelope Jones, or you will be letting yourself* **DOWN**." And so I say, "*I would not say 'I would not do that if I were you', Bridget Grimes, because* **YOU** *are letting* **YOURSELF** *down*."

And then everyone goes crazy with who is letting who down, e.g.:

a) Brady O'Grady says if Cherry Scarpelli does not give him a wintergreen mint then she is letting **PRINCE WILLIAM** down (because she is very **BIG** on Prince William).

ii) Cosmo says if Henry Potts does not stick his hand in the fly swimming pool then he is letting **ALL THE INSECTS IN THE WORLD** down.

3. Henry Potts says if Cosmo does not sacrifice himself to Minimus Mayhem then he will be letting **THE HEROBOTS** down.

And then Bridget Grimes is crying because she has slipped on the fly swimming pool and knocked her head on the lemonade machine, which makes a pingy noise and my coin falls out, which is a **MIRACLE** and I say,

Which is when Miss Patterson says in fact we are **ALL** letting **HER** down and if we do not sit down and also stop fiddling with things then Dwayne Eggs will turn the **SPEEDY SUPERBUS** around this very minute and it will be litter-picking for all of us. And **NO ONE** is very happy about this, especially Dwayne, who says he is meeting his friend Ant the Plank at the museum so he will not be turning anything around until at least 11:30. So we do all sit down and I don't even test the sprinkler system in case of **FIRE** although I would very much like to.

But when we get to the museum I am glad I did not do any testing because almost immediately I am **FULL OF WONDER**, because right inside the front door is a real actual stuffed walrus and I am very **BIG** on walruses (because they have tusks, and skin like Mrs. Butterworth at the general store or like leather handbags). And I am just about to pet it to see if it feels like Mrs. Butterworth or a handbag, because Mom did not say I could not **PET** artifacts, when Miss Patterson says, "Do not even **THINK** about it, Penelope Jones, we are not here to look at walruses, we are here to look at a cat and a coffin in a glass case," which is what we do.

And it is excellent because the room is gold and pretty dark and Cosmo says it is definitely cursed with an **ANCIENT** and **TERRIBLE** spell and if Henry Potts even **LOOKS** at the cat his nose will fall off. So Henry Potts says if Cosmo even **LOOKS** at the cat his **EAR** will fall off. And Brady O'Grady says if Alexander Pringle even **LOOKS** at the cat his **HEAD** will fall off. And then Bridget Grimes starts crying again because she **HAS LOOKED** at the cat already and she is worrying that everything is going to fall off **ANY MINUTE**.

And in fact the only person who is not **CRYING** or **GETTING CURSED** is me, which means I am not letting anyone down and Mr. Schumann would be utterly **PLEASED AS PUNCH** because I am absolutely also doing definite **WONDERING**, e.g.:

1. Is the cat named Colin?

2. Can I mummify Barry?

c) What will happen if I open the lid of the glass case?

And so in fact I **DO** open the lid of the glass case and what happens is an **ALARM** goes off and a man in a hat comes in and says,

Can't you **READ**? It says **DO NOT OPEN**.

And I say in fact I can but I did not see the sign because I was too **FULL OF WONDER**.

Which is when Miss Patterson says we are **ALL** letting her down, except for **ME** because I have let **MYSELF** down too, and it is back to the big room with the walrus after all.

And then Henry Potts is whining because he says walruses with tusks are not as full of **WONDER** as cats with curses. Only Cosmo says his mom Sunflower says **EVERYTHING** is full of **WONDER**, even things like mud, you just have to **LOOK PROPERLY**. And Miss Patterson says for once Sunflower is right, and Cosmo is **PLEASED AS PUNCH** because that almost never happens.

And then he is **DOUBLY** pleased because Miss Patterson says everyone has to find something that is **INTERESTING** in the big room and write it down and Mr. Schumann can be the judge of which is **MOST** interesting when we get back, only there is to be **NO OPENING OF CASES**. And then everyone is running around like **CRAZY** but **NOT OPENING CASES** and we are finding all sorts of interesting things, e.g.:

a) A monkey with his eye fallen out

b) A bent coin

3. Half a fossilized fish

Eyeball

But I am still absolutely **INTERESTED** in the walrus and it is not **EVEN** in a case so I think I will just touch it now because Mr. Schumann will utterly want to know if it feels like Mrs. Butterworth. Only then something definitely **CURSED** happens which is that a tusk just **FALLS OFF** and I didn't even wiggle it more than two times. And so I am about to stick it back in the hole in the walrus's mouth when I see the man with the hat coming completely quickly in my direction, so I think it is not a good time to be sticking tusks back on walruses (even ones that have not been glued properly) and so I put it in my pocket for later and go completely quickly in the other direction to look at a knife with a ruby in the handle.

Only what happens is I am so **FULL OF WONDER** at the knife with the ruby in the handle that I completely forget about the tusk. And when Miss Patterson says it is time to get back on the Speedy Superbus and there had better be twenty-seven of us and I can do the counting as I absolutely need to practice my math, I am so **FULL OF WONDER** at being allowed to count that I completely forget about the tusk again.

Only when we get back to school it also turns out that I forgot about Alexander Pringle, who was in the museum gift shop buying an eraser shaped like a beehive. Only I still counted to twenty-seven people which I say is a **CURSE**, but which Miss Patterson says is an **OVERSIGHT** and it is not the same thing and it is because I counted her by mistake and so she is **SICK AND TIRED**.

And Dwayne Eggs is **SICK AND TIRED** because he has to go back to the museum on the Superbus to get Alexander Pringle, only he wants to play Nintendo. But the most **SICK AND TIRED** is Mr. Schumann when I ask if Dwayne can possibly take back the walrus tusk that I have just miraculously found in my pocket as well. He says it is **CURTAINS** for field trips until I can learn to count and also to not mess with museum exhibits and no I have not won the "most interesting" competition, Cherry Scarpelli has won it with a bucket made of bronze.

Daisy says, "*It is all your fault, Penelope Jones, you are such a complete* **MORON**." Only I say I am not a **MORON**. I am just **TOO FULL OF WONDER**. And sometimes that is an utter **CURSE**.

And for once Mom agrees.

Penny Dreadful's
Top **5** Tips for Survival

Sometimes it is very **ARDUOUS** being a

MAGNET FOR DISASTER. Especially if

you are extra specially magnetic, i.e. like me.

But even though it is **ARDUOUS**, it is also

very **INFORMATIVE**,

i.e. I have learned

some important

TOP TIPS

about how to

avoid complete

CATASTROPHE.

Number 1

Get a DISGUISE

It is completely important not to look like me, i.e. Penelope Jones, when I am being very magnetic, e.g. accidentally knocking over a teetering pile of envelopes in the general store. So sometimes I dress up as Cosmo, i.e. in a Jedi outfit and rainboots, because it completely confuses Mrs. Butterworth's beady eye and however hard she **RACKS** her brain she is **DISCOMBOBULATED** as to who to shout at.

Another good disguise is dressing up as a burglar, because burglars wear balaclavas which **COMPLETELY** cover up their face.

Although it is possible you would get shouted at for being a burglar anyway.

Number 2
Collect COLLATERAL, i.e. money

Coins are **EVERYWHERE**, e.g. on the ground outside the general store, down the back of the sofa and mostly in Dad's pants pocket.

Collect them **ALL** because you never know

when you might need them for:

1. Paying people back, e.g. your Aunt Deedee

when you have accidentally broken a glass

vase or called Russia, for instance.

b) Buying essential supplies

like cookies or licorice sticks.

iii. Playing ludo, because you have

used the actual plastic counters to

flick at your mortal enemy.

Number 3
Be PREPARED for EVERY EVENTUALITY

DISASTERS are **EVERYWHERE** and you never

know when you might be super-magnetic,

so it is completely important to have a box

of useful things for **EVERY EVENTUALITY**,

i.e. anything, e.g.:

a) **COLLATERAL** (see above).

2. **A DISGUISE** (see above).

3. **COOKIES** (for **ARDUOUS**

JOURNEYS).

4. A bottle of dishwashing liquid and a

sponge (for when you have spilled something, or

accidentally drawn some Roman soldiers

marching along the kitchen wall).

e) A flashlight (for when you have

accidentally blown up the vacuum cleaner by

trying to suck up the dishwashing liquid, and

all the lights have gone off).

Number 4

Find a TRUSTY SCAPEGOAT

This means someone else to **BLAME**, e.g. in our house everyone mostly blames me, even though it is not usually my fault, it is that I am a **MAGNET FOR DISASTER**. So I usually blame Barry the cat, because he is most often eating things that are **NOT** cat food. E.g. when Daisy said, "Where is my last chocolate-covered cherry, Penelope Jones? I **KNOW** it is you who has eaten it," I said, "But in fact maybe it is not I, it is **BARRY**, because he completely **ADORES** cherries and chocolate, so ha!"

Number 5

Get a FAITHFUL FRIEND

If you are very magnetic like me, it is

COMPLETELY important to have a faithful

friend, which is not the same thing as a

scapegoat, and is also not the same as a dog,

(especially not one that isn't yours but which

you have found outside the general store only it

is not lost at all) but e.g. Cosmo Moon Webster.

Because faithful friends will always stand up

for you, even when you have accidentally

exploded pudding in their microwave,

and even if they are a boy

and exactly a week

older than you.

My
Faithful Friend

Joanna Nadin

wrote this book –
and lots of others
like it. She is small,
funny, clever,
sneaky and musical.
Before she became a writer, she wanted to be a
champion ballroom dancer or a jockey, but she
was actually a lifeguard at a swimming pool,
a radio newsreader, a cleaner in an old people's
home, and a juggler. She likes peanut butter on
toast for breakfast, and jam on toast for dessert.
Her perfect day would involve baking, surfing,
sitting in cafes in Paris, and playing with
her daughter – who reminds her a lot
of Penny Dreadful…

Jess Mikhail

illustrated this book.

She loves creating funny

characters with bright

colors and fancy patterns

to make people smile. Her favorite

place is her tiny home, where she lives with her

tiny dog and spends lots of time drawing,

scanning, scribbling, printing, stamping, and

sometimes using her scary computer. She loves to

rummage through a good charity shop to find

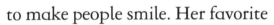

weird and wonderful things. A

perfect day for her would have to

involve a sunny beach and large

amounts of spicy foods and ice

cream (not together).

For all the small Masons, who are full of
BRILLIANT IDEAS™

First published in the UK in 2012 by Usborne Publishing Ltd., Usborne House, 83-85 Saffron Hill, London EC1N 8RT, England. www.usborne.com

First published in America in 2015 AE.

PB ISBN 9780794529918
ALB ISBN 9781601303530
FMAMJJASOND/15 00843/8
Printed in Dongguan, Guangdong, China.